ve SF CA 94118

94315

W9-ATZ-565

DATE DUE

Brodart Co.   Cat. # 55 137 001   Printed in USA

2020

Eloise Greenfield
GRANDPA'S FACE

ILLUSTRATED BY
Floyd Cooper

Penguin Young Readers Group

Text copyright © 1988 by Eloise Greenfield
Illustrations copyright © 1988 by Floyd Cooper
All rights reserved. This book, or parts thereof, may not be reproduced
in any form without permission in writing from the publisher.
A PaperStar Book, published in 1996 by The Putnam & Grosset Group,
345 Hudson Street, New York, NY 10014.
PaperStar is a registered trademark of The Putnam Berkley Group, Inc.
The PaperStar logo is a trademark of The Putnam Berkley Group, Inc.
Originally published in 1988 by Philomel Books, New York.
Published simultaneously in Canada
Manufactured in China

Library of Congress Cataloging-in-Publication Data
Greenfield, Eloise. Grandpa's face/Eloise Greenfield;
illustrated by Floyd Cooper.   p.   cm.
Summary: Seeing her beloved grandfather making
a mean face while he rehearses for one of his plays,
Tamika becomes afraid that someday she will lose his love
and he will make a mean face at her.
[1. Grandfathers—Fiction. 2. Actors and actresses—Fiction.]
I. Cooper, Floyd, ill. II. Title. PZ.&. G845Gs 1988
[E]—dc19 87-16729 CIP AC
ISBN 978-0-698-11381-7

33 35 37 39 40 38 36 34

To my mother, Ramona,
whom I love,
to my grandfather C.D.,
whom I look up to,
and to my aunt Emma who
both inspired and encouraged me.
—FC

Tamika loved her grandpa. She loved the quiet way he talked and the surprise of his loud laughter. She loved the stories he told, long stories that he sang and talked, a little bit each day, until he reached the end. Most of all, Tamika loved Grandpa's face.

Grandpa's face told everything about him. It was always changing from glad to worried to funny to sad. Grandpa could ask a question without saying one word, and even when he was mad with Tamika, his face was a good face, and the look of his mouth and eyes told her that he loved her.

"You shouldn't have done that, Tamika," Grandpa would say. And Tamika would tell him she was sorry, and then she would kiss the sturdy brown of his face.

Sometimes Tamika and Grandpa would go out together, just the two of them. They would leave Mama and Daddy at home and go for a walk. A talk-walk, Grandpa called it. They'd walk through the park, or just around the neighborhood, and talk about things they saw and felt and remembered.

In the summer Grandpa was an actor, and some Saturday afternoons he and his friend, Ms. Gladys, would take Tamika to the theater to watch him act on the stage, if Mama and Daddy said the play wasn't too grown-up.

The theater was Tamika's favorite place to go. Make-believe things happened there. She would sit in the front row and watch Grandpa turn into another person, changing his face and the way he walked and talked and sang. And even when he turned into somebody else's grandpa, Tamika didn't mind. It looked true and it felt true, but she knew it was just a play, and when it was over and all the actors came out to bow, and bow, and wave, she would clap so hard her hands hurt.

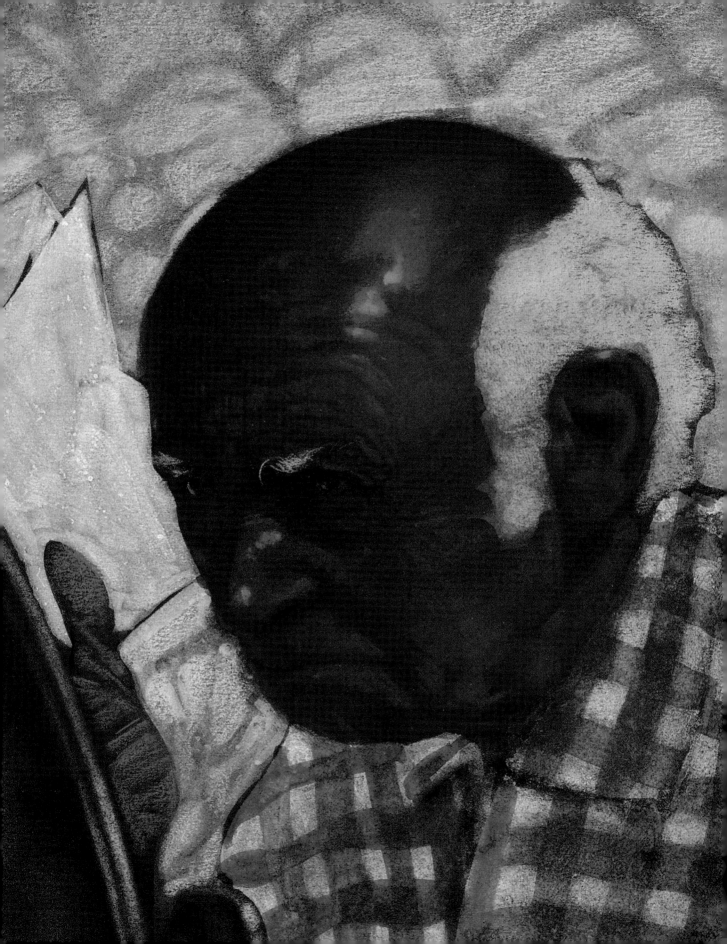

One day, Tamika went to Grandpa's room to ask for a story. She stopped at the door because Grandpa was rehearsing. He had his book in his hand and he was reading his lines aloud. Then he stopped reading and looked in the mirror, slowly changing his face into a face that Tamika had never seen before. It was a hard face. It had a tight mouth and cold, cold eyes. It was a face that could never love her or anyone.

Tamika stood watching, as Grandpa changed his face back and read some more lines from his book. Then she went to her room and sat on the bed. Her stomach was filled with scared places that made her want to cry. She had not known that Grandpa could look like that, and now that she did know, she couldn't be sure that he might not someday look at her with that face that could not love.

She got out her jigsaw puzzle and played with it quietly until Mama and Daddy had finished cooking dinner. Then she washed her hands and sat down at the table, but she didn't feel like eating. She felt like doing bad things, all the things that Grandpa didn't like. So she made a hill out of her mashed potatoes and let her green peas roll down the hill.

"Stop playing in your food, Tamika," Mama said, "and eat your dinner."

Tamika looked at Grandpa's face, and it was still the face she knew. So she put a forkful of greens in her glass and watched her water turn a muddy green. Then she tapped on her plate with her spoon while the grown-ups were trying to talk.

"I think you want to leave the table," Daddy said.

"No, Daddy," Tamika whined.

"I think you'd better, Tamika," Daddy said. "Go to your room now, and you can eat by yourself later."

Tamika began to cry a little. She looked at her mother
and father, but when she started to look at Grandpa,
too, she felt the scared places in her stomach again, and
she was too afraid to look. Then she cried harder. She
stood up, crying loud and not watching what she was
doing. Her hand bumped her glass and knocked it over,
sending green water spattering onto Grandpa's shirt
and across the tablecloth.

"Tamika, what in the world . . ." Grandpa said.

Tamika turned and looked at him then, expecting to see the face she had seen in the mirror. But it was Grandpa's face she saw. Grandpa's mad face, but still it was the one that loved her.

Mama and Daddy looked worried. "Tamika," Mama said, "what's this all about?"

Tamika hung her head and didn't answer.

"Stop crying now," Daddy said. He wiped her face while Grandpa went to change his shirt.

Then Grandpa came back and took her by the hand.
"Let's go," he said. "Time for a talk-walk."
   Tamika and Grandpa walked toward the park,
holding hands.

"Now, tell me what's wrong," Grandpa said.

Tamika's hand felt good inside Grandpa's, but she wasn't sure she felt like talking. She watched the lines in the sidewalk for a little while. Then she said, "You have another face, Grandpa."

"I do?" Grandpa said.

"Uh huh, I saw it in the mirror," Tamika said. "And it's a real mean face, too."

They sat down on the grass and Tamika let the words spill out. "The mouth is mean and the eyes are mean, and I don't like that face, Grandpa," she said.

"But that's just pretending, Tamika," Grandpa said. "You know that."

"But it might not always be pretend," Tamika said.

Grandpa thought for a moment. "Oh, I see," he said. Then he put his hands around Tamika's face and made her look at him. "I love you," he said. "I could never, ever, look at you like that. No matter what you do, you hear?"

"You sure?" Tamika said.

"As sure as I am that you love me," Grandpa said.

Tamika knew she was safe then, safe enough to hug Grandpa and kiss the sturdy brown of his face.

Grandpa hugged her back. "Let's go home, now," he said.

On the way home, Grandpa stopped to talk to an old friend, but Tamika didn't pay any attention to what they were saying. She was much too busy watching a wave of laughter as it spread across her grandpa's face.